Jungle Jam Chapter Books

King Liar

Jungle Jam Chapter Books: King Liar © MMII by Fancy Monkey Studios, Inc.

Visit us at FancyMonkey.com.

"King Liar" and "How Green Was My Sully"
written by Jeff Parker
illustrations by Matthew Bates
cover design by Messy Studio, Los Angeles

ISBN 1-59269-002-5

Manufactured in the United States of America

King Liar

Proverbs 6:17

Chapter One

The Bible says in Proverbs 6:17 that God hates a lying tongue. In fact, the Jungle Jam gang isn't fond of it either. Reynold the warthog learned that lesson in a most unusual way.

It all started one morning when Reynold woke up. He stretched and looked around his crude sleeping fort. He had made it himself. But Reynold wasn't a very good fort-builder. So it looked, well, like a mess. "Like a wood pile with a door," he grumbled. He pulled on the knob and the door broke off in his hand.

"Like a wood pile."

He tried to cheer himself up by sliding into his mud hole. Just as he did, he heard splashing and laughing. It came from the swimming hole on the other side of the brush. Reynold walked closer and then peeked though the cattails.

"Cannonball!" said Sully the aardvark, jumping in and making a great splash.

"Good one," said Millard the monkey, floating on an inner tube. "The wave you made almost knocked me right out of the water!"

Reynold wanted to play in the swimming hole. It looked fun. But he wasn't a very good swimmer and the other animals made too many waves. Reynold turned and walked back to his mud hole. "Let's face it," he said. "Floating in mud is a lot easier than floating in water." As he walked past his fort, part of a wall crumbled.

"Rotten old sleeping fort," he said, sliding into the mud. He put a couple of cucumber slices over his eyes and tried to relax.

He heard the gang laughing and having fun in the swimming hole. "I want to go swimming," he said. "It would sure feel good to rinse all this mud off. Sometimes there's a dirt-like quality to mud. It's hard to explain."

The longer he sat, the grumpier he became. "I don't want to be stuck in the mud next to this lousy fort. I want to breathe fresh air and swim in clean water for a change. Besides, there's a rock poking me in the back."

Then he grew very excited. "I want to learn to do the backstroke!" But as quickly as it came, his excitement faded. "I'll never be able to swim in that wonderful swimming hole."

Out of the blue, Reynold heard what sounded like a huge, roaring ape behind him! He quickly turned to see what it was.

It wasn't an ape. It was his sleeping fort. A big part of the roof had just crashed to the ground.

Reynold shook his head sadly. "My life is terrible. And what an awful noise."

Then he got an idea.

Chapter Two

Nozzles the elephant, Racquet the skunk, Sully, Millard, and the rest of the Jungle Jam gang swam and played at the swimming hole. Gruffy Bear stood nearby barbecuing. "I know we just finished breakfast," he said. "But no sense waiting until the last minute for lunch."

"Bear," said Millard, "I like the way you think." He and Sully sat on an inner tube. They made it rock up and down like a teeter-totter. "Whoa! Weeee!" said Millard.

"Whoa! Weeee!" said Sully, laughing. Then, suddenly, he stopped laughing and rocking.

"Come on, Sully," said Millard. "I can't 'Whoa! Weeee!' all by myself." Sully said nothing. He just stared. "Wait a minute," said Millard. "Yes, I can." He started to make the inner tube rock again, but Sully stopped him.

"L-l-l-look," said Sully, pointing. The gang turned around. There in the brush was a huge angry-looking creature!

"Oh no!" said Gruffy. "It's a giant baboon! And he looks mean!"

"Actually," said Millard, "that's a giant ape. You see, a baboon --"

"Never mind, Millard!" said Gruffy.

"Rrrroooaarrr!" said the ape.

"But you're right about the mean part!" said Millard. He didn't know if he should run or just cry.

"Rrrroooaarrr!" said the hairy ape, marching right up to Millard. He decided to cry.

"Stop crying right now," said the ape. "I'm not mean."

"You're n-n-not?" said Sully, his teeth chattering with fear.

"No."

"Then what brings you here?" said Nozzles. He tried to hide his shaking knees.

"I'm the king of the jungle!" said the ape.

Millard stopped crying. "You are?"

"Yes!" said the ape. "And as my royal subjects, you must all do as I say."

Sully looked confused. "Isn't the king of the jungle supposed to be a lion?"

"Quiet!" said the ape king, showing his large and powerful teeth. "Now, I command that only I may swim today."

"What?" said Nozzles. He was wearing his polka-dot water wings, his goggles and a huge nose plug.

"That's right," said the ape. "In fact, no one shall even come close enough to see my royal-ness swimming!"

Gruffy looked like he'd bitten into a piece of bad fruit. "'My royal-ness?' Did he just say, 'My royal-ness?'"

14.

"Quiet!" said the ape king. "Off with you! It is time for my royal swim."

The ape watched as the gang started to leave, grumbling as they went. "No swimming? This is outrageous!" They kept walking until the ape could no longer see them.

Then he looked around. He unzipped a zipper down his back. A much smaller animal wiggled his way out of the ape suit.

Reynold the warthog.

"Cannonball!" said Reynold, swirling the tip of one toe in the water.

Chapter Three

Reynold spent a fine day playing in the swimming hole. Of course, not being a very good swimmer, he was careful to only go in up to his knees. Even so, swimming in water was a nice change from wallowing in mud. He played the whole day. On his way home, he had a thought.

"Only one thing could make this day more perfect," said Reynold. "A peanut butter sandwich."

Then he remembered he was the king. At least that's what he'd made everyone think. He might not even have to make the sandwich himself.

The next day, Reynold dressed up in his ape suit. He went back to the swimming hole. "Roarrrr!" He didn't really know how else to start his speeches. And roaring worked well the day before. "Today," he said, "your king wants the swimming hole to himself again."

"What?!" said Nozzles. He had his favorite beach towel around his neck, carried his extra-large blow-up ducky, and had put a whole bottle of sunscreen on his trunk.

"What's more," the ape said, "your king commands you to make him lunch."

"You mean with high stacks of sliced melons?" said Gruffy.

"And peaches and grapes and fruits of all kind?" said Millard.

"Swiss and other types of cheese," said Sully.

"An ice sculpture!" said Racquet.

"And a cart with every kind of soft drink," said Nozzles.

"Great," said the ape. "Except change all that stuff to peanut butter sandwiches. But keep the ice sculpture. And make it a sculpture of a peanut butter sandwich."

Nozzles shook his head. "This guy just doesn't let up."

"Yeah," said Gruffy. "But you've got to love his taste in food."

The animals made the feast. They took it to the swimming hole and left. When they were gone, Reynold once again took off his ape suit. He happily waded into the water. This time he went in all the way up to his waist.

Reynold played in the water all morning. Then he decided it was time for lunch. The peanut butter sandwiches really hit the spot.

The next day, the ape again ordered everyone away from the water.

"You've got to be joking!" said Nozzles.

18.

He was carrying a deck chair, his favorite beach ball, and a special radio that played nothing but surf tunes.

"And bring me my sandwiches!" said the ape.

When they had finished making the feast, the ape said, "Follow me."

"Why?" said the animals.

"Today I need you to build a fort. But not just any fort. I want you to build me the greatest fort ever!"

Chapter Four

"Right here!" said the ape.

"At Reynold's mud hole?" said Racquet. "Why would you want to build a fort here?"

"On the other hand, it is mud-front property," said Nozzles.

The ape pointed to the broken-down fort. "In fact, that's the perfect spot."

"But that's Reynold's sleeping fort!" said Millard.

"He built it himself," said Sully.

20.

Gruffy watched as the front porch fell off. "That's Reynold's work all right."

The ape said, "You'll have to tear it down to make room for the new fort."

"Or we could just wait a minute," said Gruffy.

Sully looked around. "Speaking of Reynold, where is he?"

"Reynold is, um, on vacation," said the ape. "When he comes back, he can have the new fort."

"He can?" asked Nozzles.

"Yes," said the king. "And I shall return to my castle."

"Wait a minute," said Gruffy. "I see what's going on here."

"Y-you do?" said the ape.

"Yes. You want us to tear down Reynold's fort. And in its place, build the greatest fort ever. Then when you leave, Reynold can live in it."

"Not quite," said the ape. "No, wait. That's it exactly."

Gruffy leaned over to Racquet.

"Nothing gets by the old Grufster."

"You know, mister king?" said Sully. "You're not such a bad guy after all."

Reynold went back to the swimming hole. He slipped out of his hot ape suit and into the cool pool. He waded in up to his neck. It felt good, almost like he was swimming.

After awhile he got out and had lunch. The peanut butter sandwiches tasted extra yummy. The grape jelly was a nice touch. As he ate, Reynold heard the animals in the distance. They were tearing down his old sleeping fort.

After lunch, Reynold went back into the water. But this time, he went all the way in. His feet didn't even touch the bottom. "I can swim! I can swim!" said Reynold. And he could.

At least he could move his arms enough so he wouldn't sink.

But he couldn't make himself move

forward or backward. He was only able to keep his head above water. And he quickly discovered something important.

He couldn't get back to the edge.

"Uh oh," said Reynold. "This could be bad."

He tried everything he could think of to make himself move. Nothing worked. His arms grew tired.

Reynold started to panic.

"Gruffy! Sully! Millard! Nozzles!" he yelled. They couldn't hear him. "Racquet!" They were too busy tearing down his sleeping fort. It was very loud. Reynold had to think of something fast.

"Help!" he yelled. "Help! Help! Help!"

Reynold wasn't known for his fast thinking.

Chapter Five

The animals finally finished tearing down Reynold's sleeping fort. Gruffy said, "Let's stack everything over to one side. We'll try to reuse as much as we can."

"Help! Help, help!" said a voice in the distance.

"Did you hear that?" said Sully.

"Help! Help!" said the voice.

"It sounds like it's coming from the swimming hole!" said Nozzles.

26.

The animals dropped their hammers and boards. They ran as fast as they could. When they got to the swimming hole, they saw Reynold.

"Help!" said Reynold. His arms grew more and more tired. He began to sink lower in the water.

"Reynold!" said Sully. "When did you get back from vacation?"

"And don't you know you're disobeying the king's orders?" said Gruffy.

"Good thing the king isn't around to see this," said Millard.

Then Sully saw the ape suit lying on the ground. "Uh-oh!"

"Uh, guys," said Reynold, his mouth barely above water.

"Quiet!" said Millard. "Can't you see the king is napping?"

"Huh?" said Reynold. "Oh! Napping. Of course. Help me out of here. We'll leave before he wakes up."

"Wait a minute," said Nozzles. He walked over to the ape suit.

"Nozzles, no!" said Reynold. "Stay back! You'll wake the king!"

"This is no ape king," Nozzles said. "This is just an ape suit."

"You're right!" said Racquet.

"I don't think there's an ape king at all," said Nozzles. "I think someone was lying to us." Nozzles looked at Reynold, still in the water.

"That's awful!" said Racquet. "Who would do that?"

"Maybe someone who wanted the swimming hole all to himself," said Nozzles.

"Who would want that?" said Sully. "It's more fun when we all swim. We splash and make waves and laugh really hard together."

"Uh, guys?" said Reynold, sputtering.

"Maybe someone who didn't know how to swim very well," said Nozzles. He nodded his head toward Reynold.

28.

Millard scratched his ear. "I don't know anyone who would lie to us."

"I don't either," said Sully.

"This is a tough one," said Gruffy. "I was going to say Nozzles. Then I remembered he could swim."

"Thank you, Gruffy," said Nozzles.

The gang thought about it for another moment. Nozzles nodded toward Reynold.

"Something wrong with your neck, Nozzles?" said Gruffy.

"No," said Nozzles. "Come to think of it, I did sleep a little funny last night."

"Me!! Me!!" said Reynold. "I did it! I lied to you!"

"Reynold," said Gruffy, rubbing his chin. "Hmm. I don't know. I think you can swim."

"I did it!" said Reynold. "I wanted the swimming hole all to myself. I don't know how to swim very well. So I lied to you all. I'm sorry."

"You'd better jump in and get him, Sully," said Nozzles. "He says he can't swim very well."

Sully jumped in and pulled Reynold to the shore.

"Thank you," said Reynold. "All of you. I really am sorry. I'll never lie to you again. I promise."

"We forgive you," said Nozzles.

"Of course, I still can't swim," said Reynold. "And now my fort is destroyed."

"I can teach you to swim," said Sully.

"I'll help you build a new fort!" said Gruffy.

"And I'm gonna make myself a peanut butter sandwich," said Millard.

"Millard!" said the animals.

"Okay, I'll make them for everyone!" said Millard.

The animals all went off to work on Reynold's new fort together.

After a moment, a warthog walked up to the swimming hole. He looked around. Then he unzipped a zipper down his back. Out of the warthog suit stepped a huge ape. "Roaaarrr!" he said.

And went swimming.

How Green Was My Sully

James 3:16

Chapter One

The Bible tells us in James 3:16 that "where you have envy... there you find disorder and every evil practice." Sully the aardvark learned the hard way just how dangerous envy can be.

Everyone knew that Sully had the best toy collection in the jungle. It was a fact. They actually took a poll. Sully won by a full 82%.

The gang was happy for Sully and his

toys. Sully played with them in his front yard every day.

One afternoon he thought, *I have every toy I could ever need.* That made him smile.

Just then, Nozzles the elephant walked by. Sully noticed his friend carried a box.

"What do you have there, Nozzles?" said Sully.

"Oh, hi, Sully," said Nozzles. "It's a brand new toy telescope."

"Wow!" said Sully. "What's a telescope?"

"You look through it. You can see things that are really far away," said Nozzles.

"That sounds great," said Sully.

"It's more than great," said Nozzles. "It's one of the most fun toys there is."

"Oh," said Sully.

"Well, have a good time with the best toy collection in the jungle," said Nozzles. He turned to go.

"By 82%," said Sully.

Sully looked over his toys. "Hey, why does Nozzles have a telescope and I don't?" he said.

Nozzles heard that. He turned around. "Sully, you don't envy my telescope, do you?"

"Envy?" said Sully.

"Yes. It means that you want it because I have it and you don't," said Nozzles.

"Well, yeah," said Sully. "That's not a good reason?"

Nozzles shook his head. "Sully, envy can cause you to do really bad things. Trust me. I know all about that. The danger of envy is a hard lesson to learn."

"Okay," said Sully. He didn't quite know what Nozzles meant. But he knew he sure wanted that telescope. *After all,* Sully thought, *why should Nozzles have a toy that I don't have? Oh, man. And the polls are coming out next week.* He sighed. *There goes my 82%.*

"Tell you what," said Nozzles. "I have

some chores to do. Why don't you play with my telescope for awhile? That way, you can see if you really want one."

"It's not the same as owning my very own," said Sully. "But I can pretend it's mine. Thanks, Nozzles."

Nozzles left the toy with Sully. "I'm going to play with it right now," said the aardvark. He went inside, set it up and looked through it.

"Wow!"

Sully saw a large tree he never noticed before. It looked like it was so close he could touch it. He reached out and tried. Suddenly a huge hand appeared next to the tree! It grabbed a branch! Sully screamed!

Then he looked up. He was holding the plant on his window sill. The telescope was pointed right at it. "Oh," said Sully. He laughed and let go of the plant.

Sully moved the telescope a little to one side. He looked through it again. "Hey,

there's Millard's tree house!" The monkey was
playing in front of it. "Boy, I hope he doesn't
get attacked by that giant hand," said Sully.
He dangled a giant finger over Millard's head
and grinned.

"Hey, I should get Millard to come see this telescope!" he said. "Plus, I should warn him about the giant finger." So Sully ran to Millard's.

But when Sully got there, he couldn't believe what he saw.

Millard also had a new toy.

Chapter Two

"Hey, Sully! Look at my new toy whiz car," said Millard.

"I'm looking," said Sully.

"Isn't she beautiful?" said Millard. "Candy-apple red with dual overhead rubber band engines. I got it free in a box of Sweet-Crunch cereal."

"That's nice," said Sully.

"You can collect five different cars," said Millard. "But the whiz car is the one you want."

"That's great," said Sully. "Hey, you should come to my house. I have a new telescope!"

"Wow!" said Millard. "What's a telescope?"

"Let's put it this way," said Sully. "You almost got crushed by a giant finger."

"That sounds fun," said Millard. He was busy playing with his toy car. "Rrrrrr. Rrrrrr," he said, making engine sounds with his mouth.

"So you want to play cars together?"

"Ha!" said Sully. "I think not! I'm going to go play with the telescope right now! And you'd better watch out for really giant things."

"Rrrrrr. Rrrrrr."

"Bye, Millard." Sully headed home. "It doesn't take much to make Millard happy," he said. "A silly little free car." He shook his head. "A silly little free candy-apple red whiz car," said Sully.

He stopped walking.

"Why does Millard have a red whiz car and I don't? Forget the telescope. I need a silly little free candy-apple red whiz car!"

Chapter Three

Sully ran to the store to buy a box of Sweet-Crunch cereal. He was very excited. He took the box home and opened it. Then he ate his way to the bottom. It took 14 bowls, but he made it. Sure enough, after the last bowl, he found a toy car.

But it wasn't a red whiz car.

It was a little lime-green zip car. "That's not the same thing at all," Sully said. He took it out of the box and set it on the table. The back bumper fell off. Sully tried to play with the broken car. One of the wheels wouldn't even roll.

He ran back to the store. This time he bought two boxes of cereal and raced home. One at a time, he opened them. He ate his way to the bottoms. And both times he got little lime-green zip cars.

"You wind them up and they just spin around in circles," Sully said. "Then the back bumpers fall off. What junk."

Sully ran back to the store. "Five boxes ought to do it," he said. But no red whiz car. Ten boxes. And ten green zip cars. He bought 98 boxes of Sweet-Crunch cereal. It took all the money he had. Sully ate his way to the bottom of every last one.

But no candy-apple red whiz car with dual overhead rubber band engines.

Sully didn't feel so good. He thought maybe he should give up on the whiz car. "I'll just play with the telescope," he said.

He looked through it. Millard was still laughing and playing with his toy car.

"This is horrible!" said Sully. He looked at his toys. They brought him no joy. "There's a void in my heart," he said. "A numbness. A candy-apple-red-whiz-car-shaped hole in my soul."

Sully peered at Millard through the telescope. "Look at him showing off with his precious red whiz car. He's just trying to rub it in that I don't have one. Some friend."

Sully squished Millard with the giant finger. But when Sully moved it out of the way, Millard was still playing. "I've got to have my own precious red whiz car. No matter what it takes."

"Now," he thought, "what will it take?"

Then it hit him. He took all his toys and sold them to the Jungle Pawn Shop. That got him enough money to buy 147 boxes of Sweet-Crunch. "Red whiz car, you're mine now," he said. "You've got to be in one of these boxes!"

When Sully finished the last box, he couldn't believe it. He now owned more than 262 lime-green zip cars. All of them just spun around in circles. Then their bumpers fell off.

But he didn't have one red whiz car.

Sully's tummy was huge. He could hardly stand up. He waddled over to the telescope and took a peek. Millard was still playing and laughing.

"I can't take this anymore!" said Sully.

He threw a fit. He hurled all of his

crummy lime-green zip cars into the trash. Then he flopped onto the floor. He kicked wildly in every direction. "I want that whiz car!" he shouted. "It's not fair that Millard has one and I don't!"

Sully kicked a chair. "Ouch!" he said. "Okay, maybe throwing a fit wasn't such a good idea. Now my ankle really hurts. I feel even sicker. And I still don't have a red whiz car. A fit. What a total waste of time."

Sully looked around. "More cereal," he said. "That's what I need." But there was only one thing left he could sell.

Nozzles' telescope.

Chapter Four

Sully packed up the telescope with care. "What good is pretending it's mine if I can't sell it?" he said. He tried to open the door. There were too many empty cereal boxes in front of it. He tugged and tugged. And when he did, he slipped on a box.

"Whoa!" he said.

He crashed down on his shoulder. The thud tipped over a stack of five dirty cereal bowls. They all tumbled down onto Sully's head. "Ouch! Ouch! Ouch! Ouch! Ouch!" he said. Just then, he heard a voice outside.

"Sully?" It was Nozzles. The elephant opened the door and came in. "I was coming to get my telescope and heard a crash. Are you okay?"

"I'm fine," said Sully. "If you don't count my ankle. Or my tummy. Or my shoulder. Or these five bumps on my head."

"Good, I was worried about you," said Nozzles. He helped Sully up. "Why do you have all these cereal boxes? Wow, I thought I loved Sweet-Crunch. You're quite a hearty eater."

"Thank you," said Sully.

"You know," said Nozzles, "sometimes they have prizes in these boxes."

"I've heard that," Sully said. He told Nozzles all about Millard and the toy car.

"Oooh, a red whiz car, huh?" said Nozzles. "I do love toy cars."

"I love all toys," said Sully. And he

really meant it. He rubbed his ankle, his tummy, his shoulder and the five bumps on his head. "Ow! Ow! Ow! Ow! Ow!"

Nozzles nodded. "The danger of envy's a hard lesson to learn."

"Yeah, yeah," said Sully. "Hey, I was just on my way to sell your telescope. Want to come?"

"What?" said Nozzles.

"I need money so I can buy more boxes of Sweet-Crunch," said Sully. "Come on. You can carry the telescope. It's heavy."

"It's also mine," said Nozzles. "And you're not selling it." He picked up the telescope box and held it tight. "You'll have to get the car some other way."

"What?!" said Sully. "It's like you don't even want me to have it. Come on, Nozzles. Be a pal."

Nozzles backed up to the front door. "Say, Sully, I didn't leave anything else of mine over here, did I?"

"I don't think so," said Sully. "But I'll look around."

"Oh, don't bother. Please." Nozzles stepped outside. "Bye, Sully."

Sully thought about what Nozzles said. *Some other way.*

Then Sully got an idea. He didn't like it. But it was the only way he could think of to get a red whiz car.

"I'll steal Millard's."

Chapter Five

Sully sneaked over to Millard's house. Millard was still playing in his front yard. He laughed and made engine sounds with his mouth. Sully stayed out of sight, but crept closer.

Millard coughed. Sully froze.

"I need a glass of water, Sully" said Millard. "Those engine sounds are killing my throat. Would you watch my car so nobody steals it?"

"Uh, sure, Millard," said Sully.

Millard left everything just where he'd been playing. Then he climbed up to his tree house.

Sully looked around. "Like taking candy from a baby," he said. "Or a red car from a monkey." Sure enough, on the ground in front of him was the red whiz car. It gleamed in the sunlight. Sully grabbed it. "Mine at last!" he said. Suddenly he heard a voice from above.

"What are you doing, Sully?" It was Millard.

"I've got it, Millard! Now it's mine! The greatest toy ever! Ha-ha-ha!"

"You're stealing my car?" said Millard.

"Not just any car," said Sully. "The candy-apple red whiz car! With dual over-head rubber band engines! Ha-ha-ha!"

"Oh, that," said Millard. "You can have that."

"Ha-ha... what?" said Sully.

"It's all yours, buddy," said Millard.

"Wait a minute," said Sully. "You said this was the one you want."

"That was before I got this one," said Millard. "I had to eat three whole boxes of Sweet-Crunch cereal. But I have it at last!"

"What?" Sully said.

Millard held up his new toy. "A lime-green zip car!"

Sully almost passed out. "A... zip... car?"

"I know," said Millard. "Isn't it amazing? This is the one you really want. Watch how funny it is! You push it and it zips around in circles and then the bumper falls off!" Millard cracked up laughing.

Sully watched Millard play with the car. "Be careful with that red one," said Millard. "Sometimes it leaks fluid."

"Oh, great," said Sully.

"Hey, I was just about to have a big bowl of Sweet-Crunch," said Millard. "Want one?"

"No, thanks. I better go home." Sully looked at the red car in his hand. Suddenly he didn't want it anymore. He gave it back to Millard and headed off.

As Sully limped home, he realized how foolish he'd been. Envy really was dangerous. It caused him to get a sore tummy. And to hurt his shoulder and his head and his ankle. And to almost sell a telescope that wasn't his. It even caused him to steal his good friend

Millard's whiz car.

Then Sully remembered he had sold his toys. All of his toys. The best toy collection in the jungle. By a full 82%.

He heard Millard playing in the distance. "Rrrrrr. Rrrrrr."

"I had 263 lime-green zip cars. They were just like the one Millard has," said Sully, passing some banana trees. "I threw them all away. Now I don't have any toys at all."

As he limped on, Nozzles leaned out from behind one of the trees. He had heard every word. The elephant shook his head and started to walk home. Then he stopped.

"Why does Millard have a lime-green zip car and I don't?" said Nozzles.

753 boxes of Sweet-Crunch cereal, an empty telescope box and a lot of leaky red cars later, he still didn't have one.

Indeed, the danger of envy is a hard lesson to learn.

What's round and shiny and travels in packs of four?

Jungle Jam™ CD 4-packs

Jungle Jam™ and Friends the Radio Show!
newly remastered in crystal-clear digital audio.

Each of the three CD-sets has nearly five hours
of episodes on four compact discs.
Feast on 12 radio shows per pack,
most with two different stories—
over 20 adventures per set for kids 4 through 74.
(Some material not appropriate for 75-year olds.)

Wild Times
in God's Creation
UPC 8-20265-21312-6

More Wild Times
in God's Creation
UPC 8-20265-21322-5

Even Wilder Times
in God's Creation
UPC 8-20265-21332-4

Even more Jungle Jam™ Chapter Books
Now you can enjoy a brand new series of Jungle Jam™ stories
without the use of electronic equipment!

King Liar
ISBN 1-59269-002-5

The Bear Who Wouldn't Share
ISBN 1-59269-001-7

The Monkey Who Cried Walrus
ISBN 1-59269-000-9

Plus more coming soon...

To find out the latest about Jungle Jam products
or to order visit
FancyMonkey.com
or call McRuffy Press at 1-888-967-1200